Tales of
Wisdom from
PANCHATANTRA

Om
KIDZ
An imprint of Om Books International

Reprinted in 2017

Om
KIDZ

An imprint of Om Books International

Corporate & Editorial Office
A 12, Sector 64, Noida 201 301
Uttar Pradesh, India
Phone: +91 120 477 4100
Email: editorial@ombooks.com
Website: www.ombooksinternational.com

Sales Office
107, Ansari Road, Darya Ganj,
New Delhi 110 002, India
Phone: +91 11 4000 9000
Fax: +91 11 2327 8091
Email: sales@ombooks.com
Website: www.ombooks.com

ISBN: 978-81-87107-89-7

Printed in India

10 9 8 7

Contents

The Three Crooks   5

The Turtle and the Geese   17

A Foolish Offer   31

The Barber's Folly   45

The Unfaithful Crocodile   61

The Three Crooks

Rishi was a very religious man who lived in a small village. Every morning, he would offer prayers to the Sun God.

Once a rich man from another village invited him to perform a puja ceremony at his house. After feeding him with a good meal, the rich man gifted him a plump goat.

Rishi did not want the goat to walk all the way to his village. So he left the rich man's house after thanking him and carried the goat on his shoulders.

He had to cross the forest to reach his village. On the way three crooks spotted him. They were hungry and had not eaten anything for many days. So, they decided to trick Rishi into dropping the goat.

The first crook went up to Rishi and said, "You look like a religious man. Why would you carry a dog on your shoulders?" Rishi was shocked. He replied, "Are you blind? It is not a dog. It is a goat."

The crook said, "Please continue on your journey if you believe it is a goat. But anyone can see that it is a dog."

Rishi decided to ignore his words and kept walking ahead.

A few minutes later, the second crook approached Rishi. He said, "Is it right for a man like you to carry a dead calf on your shoulders?"

Rishi was surprised as to why the goat did not look like a goat to others. So, he said, "It is not a dead calf. It is a goat young man." The crook replied, "Do you think I would waste my precious time to come and

tell you that it is a dead calf, if that was not really the case?"

Rishi now knew there was something wrong with what he was carrying. After all, two men could not be wrong.

He had taken a few more steps when the third crook came up to him and said, "Why on earth would a man carry a donkey on his shoulders?"

Now that was just the last straw! He dropped the goat on the ground and ran away screaming, "It is a ghost! It is a ghost!

It changes from a goat to a dog to a calf and
a donkey!"

The three crooks laughed as they saw Rishi
running away, leaving behind the food they
had desired.

The Turtle and the Geese

There was a lovely pool in the middle of a forest. In the pool lived two white geese and a turtle. The geese and the turtle were very good friends.

Sadly, one year, the rains failed. There was no water to be found anywhere. All the plants and trees had dried because of the heat. The pool had also completely dried.

The geese decided to leave the pool and fly away to a greener place. They told the turtle, "Dear friend, we have to give you a sad news. We have decided to fly away to another land, where water is in plenty."

The turtle replied, "My friends, we have been together for so long. How can you leave me and fly away? I will die here without the two of you."

The geese thought for long. They loved their friend, but they had no choice.

One of the geese said to the other, "Surely there must be a way out of this. What if we try to carry the turtle along with us?"

The other goose replied, "How can we? The turtle is too big to sit on our back."

The wise turtle had an answer. He said, "I have an idea! Let me get a stick. You two can hold the ends of the stick in your beaks. I will hold the centre of the stick in my mouth, and hang in the air."

One of the geese said, "That is a good idea, but it is dangerous too. If you open your mouth for any reason, you will fall down and die."

The turtle replied, "Why would I do that if I loved my life?"

So the geese held the stick in their beaks, with the turtle hanging in the centre, and flew away.

After travelling a short distance, the geese flew over a little village where some children were playing in the field.

The children looked up at the sky and laughed and screamed, "Look! Have you ever seen something like this before? Look at the geese and the turtle!"

The turtle was disturbed by all the screaming. He could not understand what was so funny about a turtle being carried to another place by two geese.

The children continued to laugh and shout! The turtle lost his patience and opened his mouth to say, "Why are all of you laughing at me?"

But, it was too late. He fell to the ground because of its foolishness, but did not die.

You know why? Because it was blessed with a hard shell.

The shell developed cracks, and it is believed that since then tortoises have had harder shells.

A Foolish Offer

Once upon a time, in a jungle lived three friends – jackal, leopard and crow. The three friends served the lion – the king of the jungle.

One day, they found a camel
wandering in the forest. One look at
the scared camel, the lion took pity
on him and said, "Do not be worried,

my friend. From today, you have me as your saviour. You can live here happily, and feed on the grass, which is there in plenty."

The camel was very happy and lived with the three friends.

Unfortunately, the lion got into a fight with a wild elephant. The elephant injured the lion badly, and he became very weak. He could not hunt for himself or the other animals who served him.

The leopard and jackal would hunt food for their master every day, but one day, they were left with nothing to hunt.

They went to the lion and said, "Master, we have searched everywhere, but could not

hunt an animal. Why don't we kill the camel and eat it?"

The lion was very angry. He roared, "Don't you remember that I promised him safety?"

The jackal replied, "My lord! You do not have to kill him. What if he offers himself

to you? If you still do not accept, then remember, you will not be able to live, and all of us will die along with you."

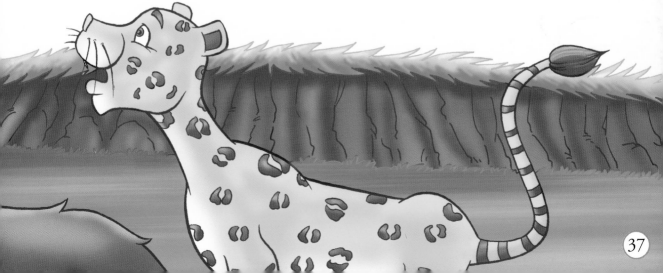

"That is even worse!" said the lion. "If the camel offers himself to me, I will kill him for food, but only if he offers..."

The jackal smiled as he had already made a plan. He called his friends together – the crow, leopard and camel. He said, "Friends,

there is no food for our master for the past few days. He may die of hunger if this continues. I think we should offer ourselves as food one by one." All the animals agreed and went to the lion.

The leopard was the first to begin. He said, "Oh lord! Please kill me and have me as food. That way, all of you will survive." The lion was shocked and said, "You are a part of my family. How can I think of such an act?"

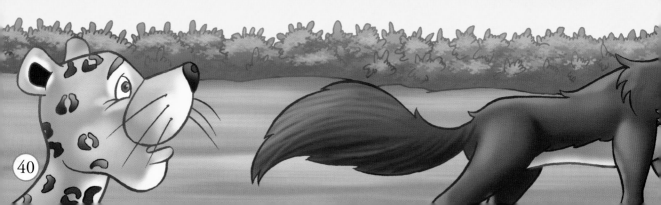

Then it was the jackal's turn. He also made the same offer as the leopard, and the lion denied. The crow was too little to be any animal's food. So, it was finally the turn of the camel.

"The lion has not killed any of his loyal servants. So why would he kill me?" thought the camel, and offered himself to the lion. But to his surprise, the moment he finished making the offer, all the animals jumped on him and killed him.

This just shows one should always be wise and never trust someone blindly.

The Barber's Folly

Hamid was a merchant. He was rich once upon a time, but had become very poor over the years.

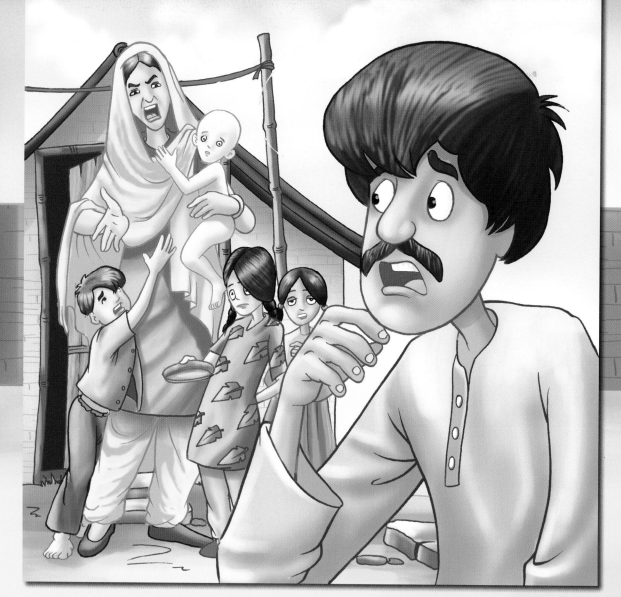

He had a family of four children and could not feed them even once a day. Every morning, his wife would tell him, "Hamid, do something! We need money. We have four children and soon they will die of hunger. Is there nothing you can do to get us food?"

Hamid would go out to find work every single day, but would never be lucky.

One night, he was tired of trying to find work, and was saddened to see his children go to bed hungry. So, he decided that he would kill himself the next day and that would be the only way to be at peace.

Hamid fell asleep with these thoughts and had a strange dream. A monk appeared in his dream. He said, "Hamid, ending your life is no solution. I appear in front of you because of the good deeds of all your ancestors. Tomorrow, I will visit your house. When you see me, strike my head with a stick and I will turn into gold."

Hamid woke up the next day, thinking it was just a dream. That day, Hamid had called the barber to his house. Just as the barber was cutting his hair, there was a knock on the door. When Hamid opened the door, he could not believe his eyes! Standing in front of him was the same monk who had appeared in his dream.

Hamid knew what he had to do. So he fetched a stick from the house and lightly struck the monk on his head. The monk turned into gold.

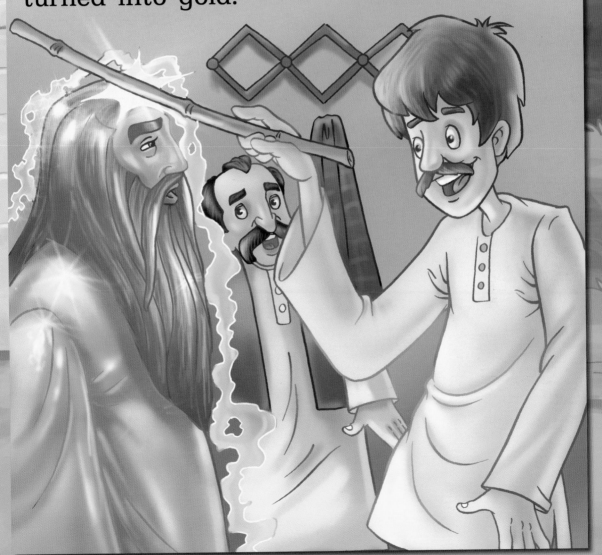

The barber who was watching all this quietly was shocked. He thought to himself, "I never knew that monks can turn into gold when they are hit on the head with a stick!"

Hamid thanked the barber, gave him a bag of gold and said, "My friend, do not tell anyone about what you saw. This is for you and your family. You can now live happily."

But the greedy barber could not sleep that night. He thought, "If all monks can be turned into gold, then I need to invite a few to my house."

So the next morning, the barber went to the monastery near his house.

He met the chief monk and said, "Sir, please visit my house tomorrow with your followers and bless my family." The monk was very pleased with the barber's invitation and agreed to visit him the following day.

The next day, the monks reached the barber's house, who locked them inside his house and before they knew, started striking them with a stick on their heads.

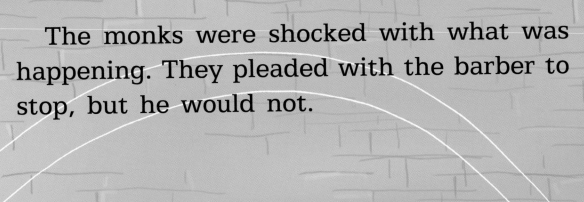

The monks were shocked with what was happening. They pleaded with the barber to stop, but he would not.

Finally, the monks managed to escape,
but were bruised black and blue all over!
The Sheriff who was passing by saw the
monks running out. He arrested the barber

for what he had done. The barber was punished to a lifetime in jail. Greed had led the barber to a life of misery.

The Unfaithful Crocodile

There lived a monkey on a big cherry tree near the lake.

One day, a crocodile came out of the lake and rested himself under the tree.

Seeing the crocodile, the monkey was scared and asked, "Who are you? What are you doing under my tree?"

The crocodile replied, "I am a crocodile and I live in the water. I came to see if there was anything to eat here."

The monkey took pity on the crocodile and said, "You are welcome. I would love to be your friend from today. Please eat this sweet fruit." The monkey threw a few cherries at the crocodile. The crocodile enjoyed eating them, and went away happily.

The next day, the crocodile came back to eat. The monkey fed his new friend a lot of cherries. This time, the crocodile carried a few cherries to his wife.

His wife was very happy to eat the cherries. She said, "If the fruit you get from the monkey is so sweet, imagine how sweet would be the heart of the monkey who eats these fruits!"

The crocodile was puzzled. His wife continued, "I want to eat the heart of your friend. I am sure it will be very sweet."

The crocodile was very angry to hear this. He said, "How could you even think of it?

The monkey is my friend. He has been feeding us every day. How could you be so cruel in your thoughts?"

The wife replied, "This is the first time you have refused me something. I am sure the monkey is a female monkey. You are in love with her, and that is why you do not want to get me her heart."

The crocodile said, "You are being foolish! I am not in love with anyone."

"Then get me the monkey's heart!" shouted his wife.

So the crocodile decided to fulfill his wife's wish and went to the tree the next day. The monkey was waiting for him.

He looked at the crocodile and asked, "Why are you looking so sad today?"

The crocodile replied, "My wife is very angry with me. She says we have not repaid your kindness. She has insisted that I take you home for lunch." The innocent monkey said, "So why are you sad about it? I cannot swim, so please carry me on your back."

Thus the crocodile and the monkey set off to the crocodile's home. After they were

mid-way in the water, the crocodile decided to tell the monkey the truth. He said, "My friend, I lied to you. Actually, I plan to kill you, and carry your sweet heart for my wife.

She thinks that your heart is sweeter than the sweet fruits you give us."

The monkey was shocked, but he decided to act calmly. He said, "You should have told me this before my friend. I would love to give my heart to you. But I keep my

heart safely on the tree, so that it does not get lost. I don't have it with me right now."

The crocodile did not know what to do. He could not go back home without the heart. So he said, "What do we do now?"

The monkey replied, "Take me back to the shore and I will quickly get my heart back from the tree." The crocodile believed him and took him back.

The moment the monkey touched the shore, he ran up to the safety of his tree, and screamed at the crocodile, "You unfaithful friend! Go away and never come back! My heart is within me, how can I keep it somewhere else – I would die!"

The crocodile knew he had been tricked, but what could he say to the monkey, because he was the one who had cheated a friend!

OTHER TITLES IN THIS SERIES

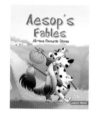 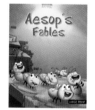    

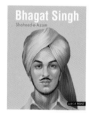 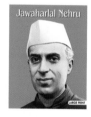   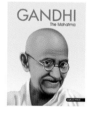 

 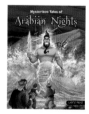  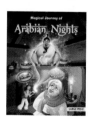 

Treasury of Tales from
PANCHATANTRA

Om
KIDZ

An imprint of Om Books International

Reprinted in 2017 by

Om
KIDZ

An imprint of Om **Books International**

Corporate & Editorial Office
A 12, Sector 64, Noida 201 301
Uttar Pradesh, India
Phone: +91 120 477 4100
Email: editorial@ombooks.com
Website: www.ombooksinternational.com

Sales Office
107, Ansari Road, Darya Ganj,
New Delhi 110 002, India
Phone: +91 11 4000 9000
Fax: +91 11 2327 8091
Email: sales@ombooks.com
Website: www.ombooks.com

ISBN: 978-81-87107-90-3

Printed in India

10 9 8 7

Contents

The Carpenter and the Monkey   5

The Cat, Partridge and the Hare   17

The Donkey Has No Brain   27

The Merchant and His Iron   41

The Crows and the Evil Snake   53

The Girl Who Married a Snake   67

The Carpenter and the Monkey

There was a group of monkeys who lived together near a small, carpenters' village.

They would feed on the nuts and bananas that the carpenters and their families would throw out to them once in a while.

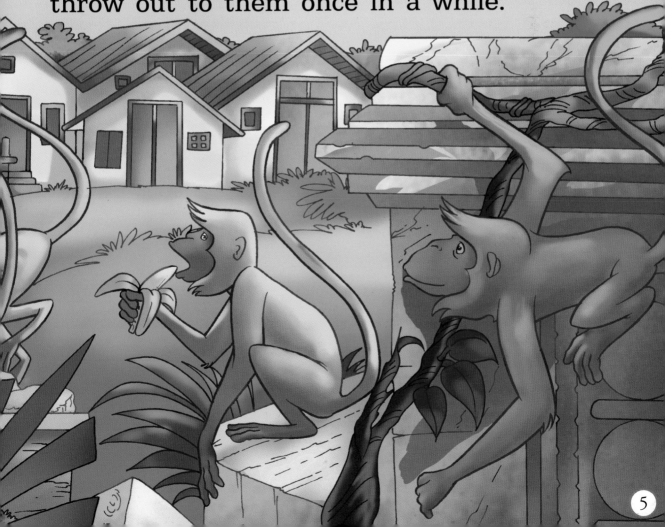

But there was one monkey who was very curious. He would always be warned by his friends, who would say to him, "Don't let your curiosity get you into trouble!"

But the monkey would always reply, "I am
more intelligent than all of you. I like to know
about new things and that is not bad at all!"
The other monkeys would shrug and move on.

One day, the curious monkey sat watching a carpenter who was splitting a log of wood with two wedges. He first drove the smaller wedge into the crack, so as to keep it open.

Then when the crack became bigger, he put
in a bigger wedge by hammering it in. After
that, he pulled out the smaller wedge that he
had put in.

The monkey thought to himself, "How interesting is that! I wish I could do it too." But, how could he when the carpenters were around? So he sat patiently, waiting for the carpenters to leave.

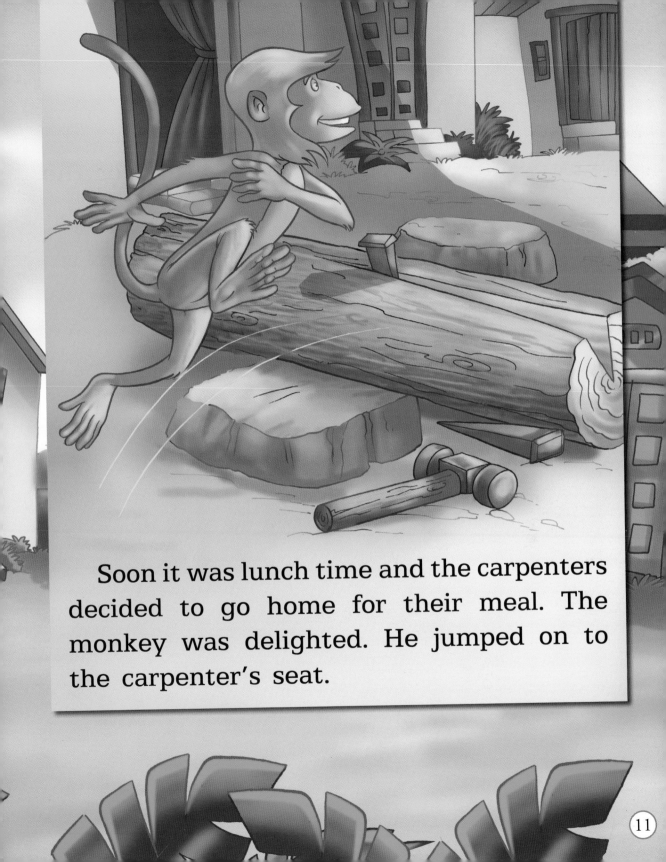

Soon it was lunch time and the carpenters decided to go home for their meal. The monkey was delighted. He jumped on to the carpenter's seat.

Unfortunately for him, his tail slipped into the crack in the wood, without his knowledge. He put in the first wedge, just the way the carpenter had done. But he had forgotten the other steps and pulled out the first wedge before hammering in the second one. The two sides of the wood instantly sprang together, and caught the monkey's tail between them!

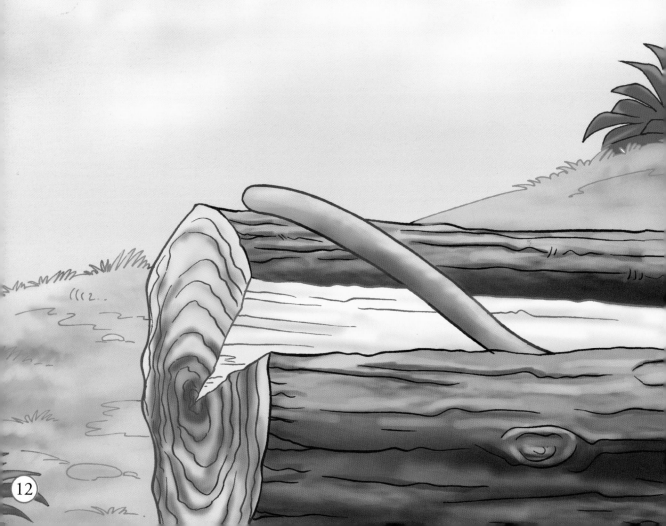

The monkey was now trapped and in pain!
Soon he could see the carpenters walking
towards him. But he could do nothing!

The carpenters saw the trapped monkey and realised what he had done. They gave him a sound beating and then let him go.

The monkey ran back to his friends, but had learnt never to meddle with other people's things!

The Cat, Partridge and the Hare

There was once a partridge who lived under a tree. He had run out of food, and decided to go and search in the nearby fields for it.

The partridge reached the fields. He was very happy to see so much food and pounced on it.

In the meanwhile, a hare had seen the
empty house under the tree, and decided
to make it his home. He started living in it.

After a few days, the plump partridge missed his home and returned. He found the hare happily living in his home!

The partridge was very angry. He asked the hare, "How can you live in my house?"

The hare replied, "Who says this is your house? I found it, and it is now mine." The partridge did not give up and continued to shout at the hare. Soon the shouting became a fight.

After hours of fighting, the hare and the partridge decided that they should seek the advice of the cat, whom every animal in the jungle listened to.

The partridge and the hare went to the cat and gave their sides of the story. The partridge said, "I left home only for a few days to find food for myself. In the meanwhile, the hare took away my house from me."

And the hare said, "I did not know it was the partridge's home. It was empty when I saw it. So it is now my home as I live in it."

The cat acted as if he could not hear. He said, "My friends, I am too old to hear you from such a distance. Please come closer and tell me your story."

The cat called the partridge and the hare closer and closer. Finally, when they were

close enough, he pounced on them and ate them up!

The foolish partridge and the hare lost their lives because they decided to seek advice from an enemy! This shows how losing your temper can make you lose all sense.

The Donkey Has No Brain

Once upon a time, there was an old lion. He was the King of the jungle, but was too old to hunt or get food for himself.

So the lion thought to himself, "I have not eaten in days. If I continue like this, I will soon die of hunger. I need an assistant to look after me."

The lion thought for hours and decided upon the fox as his assistant. The fox readily agreed. The fox's main task was to get the lion food. After hours of hunting for the right animal, the fox saw a donkey. He knew he could trick the donkey into becoming the lion's food.

The fox went up to the donkey and said, "Hello there! It is indeed a lucky day!" The donkey was puzzled at what he heard. But he was very wary of the fox, and so he took a step back.

But the cunning fox told him, "Do not be afraid! I am the King's loyal servant. The King had desired to crown you as the Chief Minister, and I have been looking for you for days." The donkey did not believe the fox. He replied, "I cannot believe a word of what you are saying. Please stay away from me." But the fox insisted that he meet the King and find out the truth for himself.

The donkey was not so sure of himself. So he decided to take a chance, and followed the fox to the lion's den. When he entered the den and saw the lion, he got very scared and ran out.

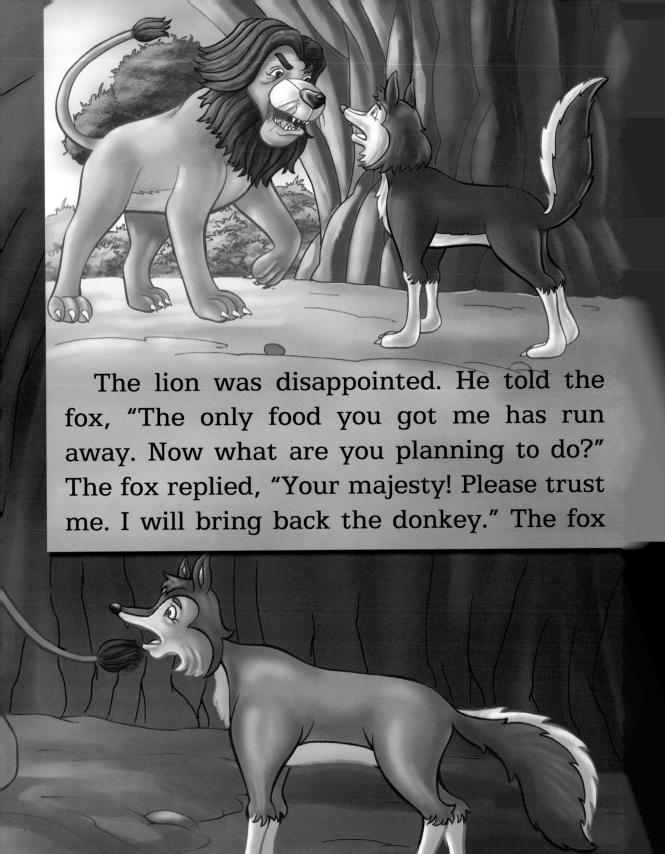

The lion was disappointed. He told the
fox, "The only food you got me has run
away. Now what are you planning to do?"
The fox replied, "Your majesty! Please trust
me. I will bring back the donkey." The fox

hurried out of the den, and found the donkey
shivering in fright. He said, "My friend, you
are putting yourself through such a fright for
nothing. If the lion had to kill you, would he

not have pounced on you? Why are you thinking of such evil things, when the lion is very kind?" The foolish donkey believed the fox. He went back into the den with the fox This time, the lion pounced and killed him.

When the lion was about to start eating the donkey, the fox said to the lion, "My lord, may I suggest that you take a bath in the river before eating."

The lion agreed and went out for a bath. The fox was now tempted to eat what was before him. So he quickly ate the donkey's brain.

The lion returned from his bath and began to feed on the donkey. But he soon realised that the donkey's brain was missing. He asked the fox angrily where the brain was. But the cunning fox replied, "My lord! Would a donkey

who agreed to come into your den the second time have a brain? It is a known fact that donkeys do not have any brain."

The lion agreed with what the fox said and continued eating.

The Merchant and His Iron

One day, a merchant went to his friend's house and left two hundred tonnes of iron with him to keep safely. The merchant said to his friend, "Please keep the iron with you safely. I am going on a long journey. I will return and sell this iron for a good price."

The friend gladly agreed and the merchant left on his journey. However, the friend was sure that the merchant would not return. So, he sold the iron for gold coins.

The merchant returned after many years. He went straight to his friend and said, "I want to thank you for looking after my iron. But now since I have returned, can I have it

back?" The friend did not know what to do. He had already sold the iron. So he lied to the merchant saying, "I had locked the iron that you had given me in a room. But, the rats ate it all up!"

The merchant knew that his friend was lying. How could the rats eat iron? But, he did not show his anger or surprise. Instead he said, "I can understand my friend. I have had rats eating up iron even before this."

The friend thought that the merchant had believed him and decided to invite him for dinner the next day.

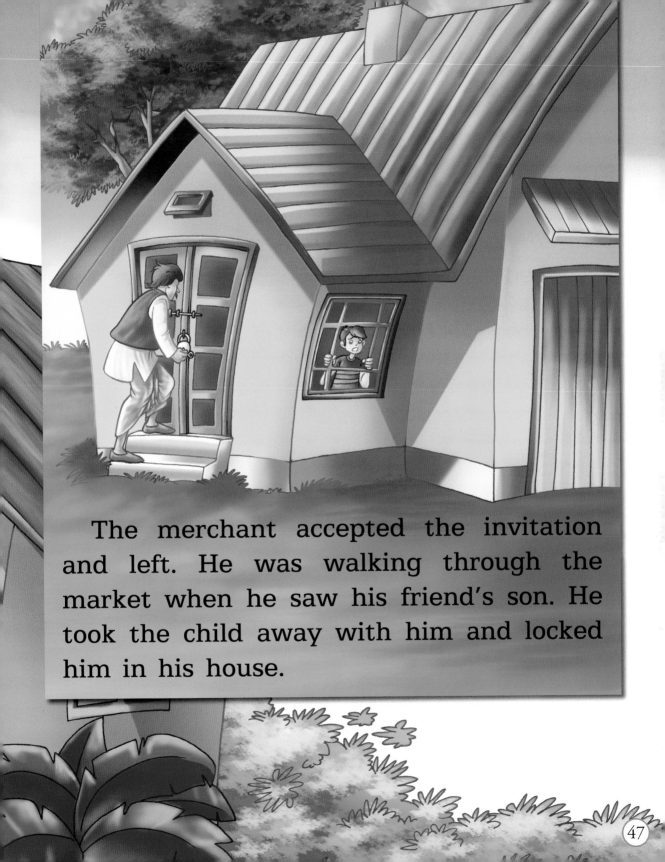

The merchant accepted the invitation and left. He was walking through the market when he saw his friend's son. He took the child away with him and locked him in his house.

The next evening he went to his friend's house. His friend opened the door, crying bitterly. He said, "My son has been missing since yesterday."

So the merchant replied, "Oh! So that was your son!" The friend looked at him with hope. He asked, "Did you see my son somewhere?"

The merchant replied, "Yes, I did. I saw a sparrow carrying a boy in its beak." The friend angrily asked, "How can a sparrow carry a five-year-old boy?"

The merchant said, "If rats can eat two hundred tonnes of iron, I am quite sure a sparrow can carry a five-year-old boy."

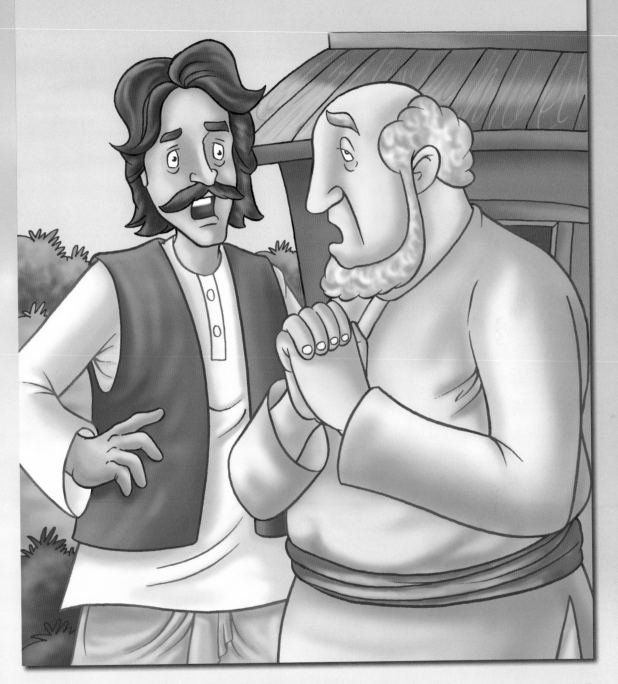

The friend realised that the merchant had tricked him. He apologised to the merchant and promised to return his money.

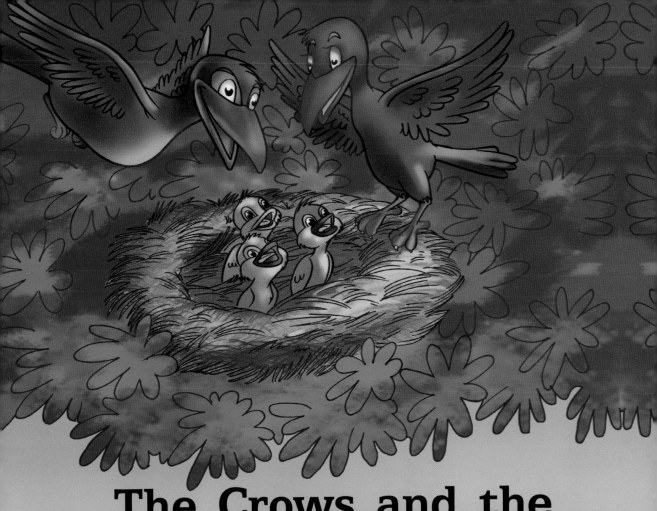

The Crows and the Evil Snake

On an old banyan tree, lived a family of crows — the father crow, mother crow and the small baby crows.

The crows lived happily on the tree, until one day, a snake came to live in a hole in the same tree.

The father crow said to the mother crow, "We have to be very careful. We now have an ugly neighbour."

Mother crow kept a watchful eye over the children every day. Soon she hatched a few more eggs.

One day, when the crows had gone out to fetch food for their children, the evil snake slithered up the tree and ate the babies.

When mother and father crow returned, they were very shocked to see that some of their babies were missing. Mother crow looked around for them everywhere, crying. But she could not find them.

Father crow knew what had happened. So he told mother crow, "Tomorrow, I'll go alone to get the food. You take care of the babies."

But, the evil snake slithered up the tree and ate the babies right in front of mother crow. She fought and tried to peck at him, but the snake was too quick. He gulped the babies and rushed back into his hole.

That evening, father crow returned home to find mother crow weeping! He was sad and angry with what the snake had done. So, father and mother crow decided to take the help of the wise old fox.

They went to him and said, "Sir, you must help us. We have lost all our children to the evil snake, who lives in the hole of our tree."

The fox thought for a long time and gave them a plan.

The next morning, the crows flew to the river bank where the ladies of the royal family would come everyday for a bath. Mother crow picked up a pearl necklace and started flying back to the tree. Father crow cawed loudly, to attract the attention of the servants. One

of the ladies, who was swimming in the river saw her necklace flying away and shouted, "Guards, What are you doing? That crow is flying away with my necklace. Catch it!"

The guards ran after the crows. Soon mother crow reached the tree and threw the necklace into the snake's hole. The servants reached the tree and put a long stick inside the hole to pull out the necklace.

Instead of the necklace, the snake came out. He hissed at them angrily. But this time, the servants were more powerful than the snake.

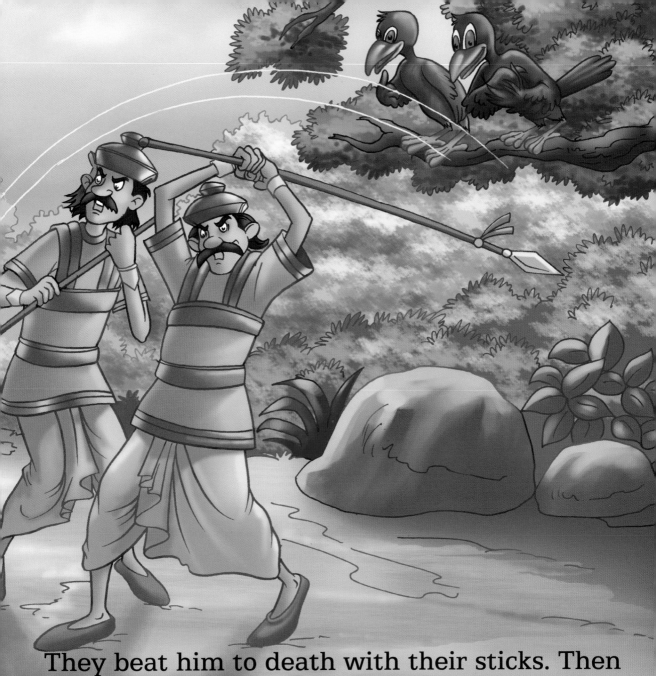

They beat him to death with their sticks. Then they picked up the necklace and walked away.

Father crow and mother crow were very happy to see that they had killed the one who had eaten up their babies.

The Girl Who Married a Snake

Long, long ago, there lived a pious man called Brahmdutt and his wife. They had no children, and so they prayed to God to bless them with a child.

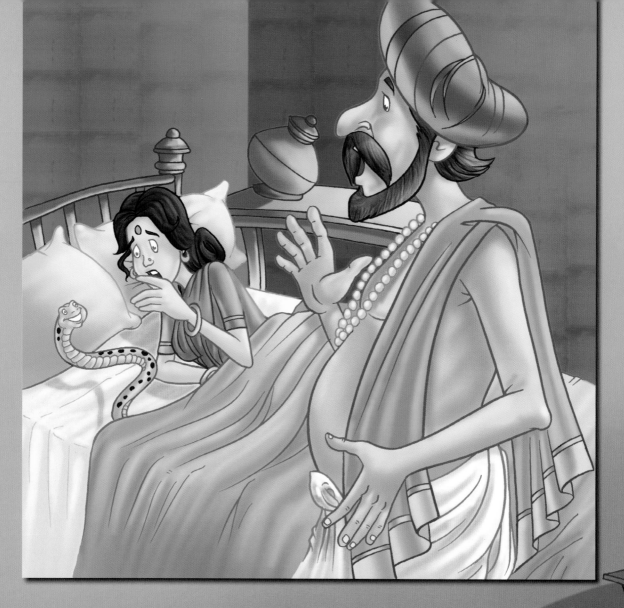

Finally, God answered their prayers and a child was born to them. But alas! The child was a snake!

All the people of the village were horrified and everyone advised them to get rid of the baby snake. But Brahmdutt and his wife refused to do any such thing. They thought of the child as a blessing and loved him dearly even though he was a snake.

Many years passed and Brahmdutt's wife worried about their son's marriage. But which girl would agree to marry a snake? She wept in front of her husband. She was upset with

him for not finding a suitable girl for their beloved son.

"You don't love our son at all," she wept.

"That's not true! I would love to see him married too. But you tell me who would marry his daughter to a snake?" he asked. Seeing his

wife so helpless and upset, Brahmdutt decided
to set out in search of a bride for his son. He
travelled far and wide, but with no success.
Poor Brahmdutt had almost given up hope.

Then he reached the big city where his
dearest friend lived. The friend was very happy

to see him but also quite surprised to see him so far from home. Brahmdutt told him that he was searching for a bride for his special son but people had only made fun of him.

His friend thought for a while and said, "Hmmm... well since I know you so well my

friend, I have no doubt your son will be the perfect match for my own daughter. So look no further! I insist you accept my daughter as your son's bride."

"Oh, but you must see my son first!" exclaimed Brahmdutt.

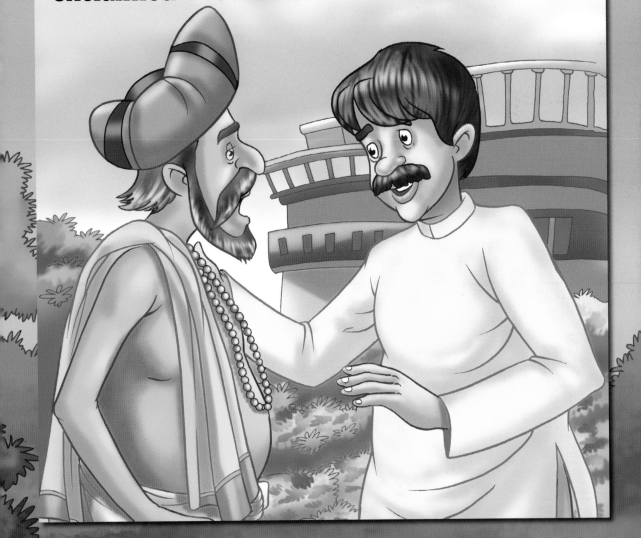

"I know your family well enough to trust you completely," replied the friend. And so Brahmdutt set out for his village along with his friend's beautiful daughter.

On reaching Brahmdutt's home, the girl soon discovered that she was to marry a

snake! But she went ahead without fear because she had to keep her father's word. She believed that the elders would have thought the best for her and she must obey them.

And so the girl and the snake were married. The girl was a devoted wife and looked after her husband well. Many days passed and life went on. Then, one night as she entered her chamber to sleep, she saw a handsome young man standing before her.

"Who are you?" she exclaimed in fright.

"Don't worry my dear, I am your husband," replied the man. "This snake

skin is a curse on me. I can now shed it at night because your love and devotion have made the curse less powerful."

The girl was overjoyed! After that, the snake would turn into a young man every night and

spend time with his wife and at day break he would slip back into the snake skin. One night, Brahmdutt heard noises in his daughter-in-law's room. Imagine his surprise when he saw his son shedding the snake-skin and changing into a handsome man! He rushed into the room and burnt the snake-skin at once!

Now the handsome young man would always remain the same, he could not be a snake again...the curse was completely broken.

OTHER TITLES IN THIS SERIES

     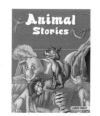

  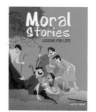   

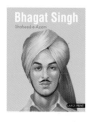 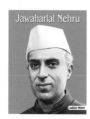 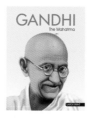   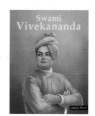

 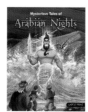